Welcome to ALADDIN QUIX!

If you are looking for fast, fun-to-read stories with colorful characters, lots of kid-friendly humor, easy-to-follow action, entertaining story lines, and lively illustrations, then **ALADDIN QUIX** is for you!

But wait, there's more!

If you're also looking for stories with tables of contents; word lists; about-the-book questions; 64, 80, or 96 pages; short chapters; short paragraphs; and large fonts, then **ALADDIN QUIX** is *definitely* for you!

ALADDIN QUIX: The next step between ready to reads and longer, more challenging chapter books, for readers five to eight years old.

Read more ALADDIN QUIX books!

By Stephanie Calmenson

Our Principal Is a Frog!
Our Principal Is a Wolf!
Our Principal's in His Underwear!
Our Principal Breaks a Spell!

A Miss Mallard Mystery
By Robert Quackenbush

Dig to Disaster
Texas Trail to Calamity
Express Train to Trouble
Stairway to Doom
Bicycle to Treachery
Gondola to Danger
Surfboard to Peril
Taxi to Intrigue
Cable Car to Catastrophe
Dogsled to Dread
Stage Door to Terror

Little Goddess Girls
By Joan Holub and Suzanne Williams

Book 1: *Athena & the Magic Land*
Book 2: *Persephone & the Giant Flowers*
Book 3: *Aphrodite & the Gold Apple*

Mack Rhino, Private Eye

Book 1: *The Big Race Lace Case*

THE BIRTHDAY CASTLE

by Dee Romito

ALADDIN QUIX

New York London Toronto Sydney New Delhi

For the wonderful Heim teachers—
Thank you for helping students construct strong foundations.
And for Heidi Ginal, for always guiding
children to build their curiosity and imaginations.

ALADDIN QUIX
Simon & Schuster Children's Publishing Division
1230 Avenue of the Americas, New York, New York 10020
First Aladdin QUIX hardcover edition May 2020
Text copyright © 2020 by Deanna Romito
Illustrations copyright © 2020 by Marta Kissi
Also available in an Aladdin QUIX paperback edition.
All rights reserved, including the right of reproduction in whole or in part in any form.
ALADDIN and the related marks and colophon are registered
trademarks of Simon & Schuster, Inc.
For information about special discounts for bulk purchases, please contact
Simon & Schuster Special Sales at 1-866-506-1949 or business@simonandschuster.com.
The Simon & Schuster Speakers Bureau can bring authors to your live event. For
more information or to book an event contact the Simon & Schuster Speakers Bureau
at 1-866-248-3049 or visit our website at www.simonspeakers.com.
Jacket designed by Karin Paprocki
The illustrations for this book were rendered digitally.
The text of this book was set in Archer Medium.
Manufactured in the United States of America 0420 LAK
2 4 6 8 10 9 7 5 3 1
Library of Congress Control Number 2020933549
ISBN 978-1-5344-5239-8 (hc)
ISBN 978-1-5344-5238-1 (pbk)
ISBN 978-1-5344-5240-4 (eBook)

Cast of Characters

Caleb Rivers: Group organizer

Mrs. Rivers: Caleb's mom

Jax Crawford: Caleb's best friend

Mr. Crawford: Jax's dad

Eddie Bell: A friend of Caleb and Jax

Junie Wheeler: A neighbor

Analise Stevens: A neighbor and the Fort Builders' first client

Mrs. Mohan: A neighbor and Kiara's grandmother

Kiara Pal: Mrs. Mohan's granddaughter

Amber & Dove: Jax's twin sisters

Mr. Rivers: Caleb's dad

Contents

1

The Big Idea

Caleb Rivers stood in the bookstore, holding a special edition of the first Castle Quest book. It was the best book series ever, and the new cover was amazing! It would look great on top of his bookshelf.

He had already saved some money from his eighth birthday last week. But it wasn't enough. He needed ten more dollars.

"Mom, please," he said. "I'll pay you back."

His mom wasn't budging. "If you earn the rest of the money, you can buy it," she said.

But he didn't have any ideas on *how* to earn the money.

"You're clever," said **Mrs. Rivers**. "You'll figure it out."

Caleb put the book back on the shelf. He started thinking of ways to earn money. But it was an empty list so far.

He thought all the way home. He thought on the two-houses-down walk to his best friend's house. (When he ran, it only took ten seconds to get there.)

"Hi, Caleb!" **Jax** kicked a soccer ball into the net. It soared right through a hole in the back.

"Hi. I need your help," said Caleb.

"For what?" asked Jax.

"The new Castle Quest special edition," he answered. "My parents said I have to save for it."

"How?" asked Jax. "A lemonade stand?" He laughed.

"Don't joke," said Caleb. "My sister made five dollars doing that."

"So where is your list of ideas?" asked Jax. "I know you made a list."

It was true. Caleb liked things organized and all in one place.

He shrugged. "That's the problem. I can't think of anything."

"What about pet sitting?" Jax asked.

"Pet sitting?" Caleb tried to imagine it. "I do like pets."

But his house was full of pets already.

"Or you could do extra chores. Or odd jobs," said Jax.

"What are odd jobs?"
asked Caleb.

"I don't know," said Jax. "But my mom has my dad do odd jobs around the house."

They both thought for a minute.

"I could use some money for a new soccer net," said Jax.

Just then, a delivery truck pulled into Jax's driveway. It said WILBUR'S APPLIANCES on the side.

"We're getting a new refrigerator," said Jax.

Caleb nodded. "Fridge boxes are the best."

The boys looked at each other.

"Are you thinking what I'm thinking?" asked Jax.

"I think I might be," said Caleb.

They ran inside.

"Dad?" Jax called. "Can we have the refrigerator box?"

Mr. Crawford smiled. He didn't even need to ask what it was for. **"Sure."**

As soon as the box was empty, the boys dragged it into the garage.

It was summer vacation, which meant they could build for as long as they wanted.

They got their supplies.

Markers.

Scissors.

Duct tape.

Extra boxes.

They started marking where the windows would go.

They measured a space for the door.

They taped up the small boxes.

The only thing they needed help with was cutting out the holes for the windows and doors. Mr. Crawford helped with that!

Two hours later, they had the perfect fridge fort.

"This looks amazing!" said Jax.

"Yeah, if only we could get paid to build box forts," said Caleb.

Jax's eyes got wide. **"That's it!"** he shouted.

"What's it?" asked Caleb.

"We could sell box forts!" Jax raised his arms in the air.

"Do you think we could do that?" Caleb asked.

Jax nodded. "Sure! But first we need a name for the business."

The boys wrote down some ideas.

Box Forts 'R' Us
Build a Fort (Not a Bear)
Dream Forts 4U
R2BoxZ

But it was the very last one that they liked the best.

"Fort Builders, Inc.," said Caleb. **"That's the one!"**

"What's the 'Inc.' for?" asked Jax.

"I don't know," said Caleb. "I think companies use it to sound fancy."

Jax took the pencil from Caleb and put a big circle around their new name.

Fort Builders, Inc.

2

Paints and Partners

Caleb and Jax had a business idea. They had a company name. They just needed customers.

But how would they let everyone know about their forts?

"We need **Eddie**," said Caleb.

Jax agreed with a nod.

They raced down the sidewalk but got there at the same time.

"Hi, guys." Their friend Eddie Bell was sitting on his steps with a sketch pad.

"Hi, Eddie. We're starting a fort-building business," said Caleb. He liked getting right to the point.

"And we need signs," said Jax.

"Ooh. I love making signs," said Eddie. "I make them for Mr. Pohlman. I get paid *and* I get free candy!"

Mr. Pohlman ran the dollar store around the corner.

"Would you make signs for us?" Jax asked. "And maybe some flyers?"

"You can help us **advertise**," said Caleb. "Get the word out."

Eddie thought about it. **"Keep talking,"** he said.

"We can't pay you anything," said Jax. "But you'd be a partner."

"And get one third of all the **profits**," said Caleb.

"Right," said Jax. "There are

three of us. We'll split the money we make three ways."

Eddie smiled. "Well, I do need a new brownie pan."

Eddie wasn't just great at art. He also made the most amazing brownies. The kind with gooey, melty chocolate chips.

He traded them for comic books at Miss Saya's bookstore, and for tokens at the local arcade. His brownies were world-famous (almost).

"Come on, Eddie," said Caleb.

"It'll be fun," said Jax.

"Okay. Count me in!" said Eddie.

The boys high-fived to make him an **official** partner.

Eddie set a blue tarp down in case it got too messy. They each took a piece of poster board.

As Jax and Caleb mixed the paints, Eddie outlined the letters.

"You paint the inside of the letters," said Eddie. "I'll draw a cool design when they're done."

Caleb painted carefully. Not one speck was outside the lines.

Jax's sign was full of paint splatters, but he liked it that way.

Just as Eddie finished outlining, Junie Wheeler from down the street walked by with her dog.

"Hey, Junie!" Jax called. "We're building box forts. Want one?"

"Sure!" Junie shouted. "That's so nice of you."

"Oh . . . we mean . . . not for free," said Caleb. **"It's our new business."** He held up his unfinished sign.

Junie's smile faded. "I don't have any money for it." She shuffled through her bag and pulled out a small container. "Can I trade you? I have a fresh batch of slime."

Jax and Caleb didn't think that trade was good at all. After Junie walked away, several other kids came by. But all the boys got were offers to trade for cookies, worms, coloring books, and half a sandwich.

"We need to get these signs done," said Eddie. "They'll help us find the right customers."

Jax dotted the period after "Inc" in green. "Yeah, but we need one more thing." He added a note at the bottom of his sign.

CASH ONLY. SORRY, NO TRADES.

3

Finding Customers

The next day, Eddie came by. "I have the signs," he said. "They finally finished drying!"

They were **BIG and BOLD** and colorful.

"These are great!" said

Jax. "We should put them around the neighborhood."

They posted the signs on lamp-posts.

They taped them to street sign poles.

Mr. Pohlman and Miss Saya even **displayed** them in their store windows.

LET US BUILD YOUR DREAM FORT!

CALL

FORT BUILDERS, INC. TODAY!

555-0108

"We should have a sample fort," said Eddie. "We can put it outside with a sign."

"That's a great idea," said Caleb. The boys ran back to Jax's house and dragged their fort to the sidewalk. Eddie put a big poster board sign in front of it.

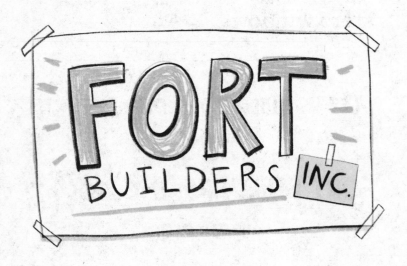

They sat and waited.

And waited.

"I don't understand," said Caleb. "Why can't we get a customer?"

"Yeah, people love forts," said Jax.

Just then, **Analise Stevens** rode by on her bike. She stopped in front of the box fort.

"Can you make a castle?" she asked.

"Sure," said Jax. **"Our fee is ten dollars."**

"I can pay you with my birthday

money when the fort is done," she said. "I'm going to need it for my party on Saturday."

"A lot of kids will be at that party," Eddie whispered to Caleb. "Everyone will know about our forts!"

"But it's already Thursday," Caleb whispered back. "That only gives us two days."

Jax stood up and shook Analise's hand. "We'll get it done," he said.

Analise didn't just want a castle fort, though.

She wanted a pink castle fort.

She wanted a pink castle fort with a pink drawbridge.

It was a big project.

The boys searched through their garages for supplies.

They found duct tape.

They even found pink paint.

What they didn't find were boxes.

"We can't build a box fort without a box," said Eddie.

"And we can't build a castle fort without a bunch of them," said Caleb.

The boys sat down on Caleb's porch.

"Someone on this block must have boxes." Jax stood up and looked down the street. "I say we go find them."

Mr. Hanifin didn't have any boxes.

Miss Tripi had just gotten rid of one last week.

Mrs. Ritz only had a small box.

But the boys weren't giving up.

"Hello, there," said **Mrs. Mohan** as they got to her driveway. "Nice day to clean the garage."

There was a pile of flattened boxes in the corner of the garage.

"Are you getting rid of those?" asked Jax.

"Those boxes are for my granddaughter," said Mrs. Mohan. "She makes all kinds of things with them."

So much for getting boxes.

"But you can have them," she said. **"I can get more."**

The easy thing would have been to say thank you and go. But Caleb thought they should do something nice for her, too.

"We can help you clean," he said. He could tell by her smile that Mrs. Mohan was happy.

Caleb organized the tools.

Eddie put the painting supplies in a bin.

Jax swept the floor with a big broom.

"Thank you, boys," said Mrs. Mohan. "Please take whatever boxes you want."

The boxes were folded flat, but they were big and heavy.

"Everybody, grab an end," said Jax.

Eddie walked backward down the street. Caleb and Jax carried the other side.

"Tell me if I'm about to run into a tree," said Eddie. "Or a big dog."

"All clear," said Jax. "Let's get this thing started!"

4

Supplies Needed!

The boys got the boxes to Caleb's garage. It was time to start building!

"How about if this box goes here?" asked Eddie. He grabbed the biggest box and put it in the center of the garage.

"Sure." Caleb helped him tape it up.

"Remember, it has to look like a castle," said Jax. He ripped a piece of pink tape. "I'll work on the pointy top."

The boys stacked and taped. They moved and lifted.

When they'd used up all the boxes, they stood back.

"It sort of looks like a castle," said Eddie.

"Nice drawbridge," said Caleb to Jax.

The next step was to paint it pink.

They set an old sheet on the ground. They gathered the brushes and paint cans.

Jax painted one box panel.

That's when Analise rode up the driveway.

"Wow," she said. "It looks great!"

The boys smiled. They'd done a good job.

"But can you move the tower over here?" She pointed from one side to the other. "And add another window over there? And the drawbridge will work, right?"

Caleb and Eddie looked at

Jax. He was the master builder, after all.

"I guess we can do that," he said. "It'll take us a little longer."

Analise patted the box fort.

"Remember, I need it by Saturday. Twelve o'clock sharp."

Analise kept looking at the fort. "You know, it would be even better with purple tape," she said. "You could line the edges with it."

Analise did not mention that before.

"We don't have purple tape," Caleb said to Analise.

"You promised me the box fort of my dreams," she pointed out. "My dream fort has purple tape."

Well, "Let us build your dream fort" *was* their **motto**.

"We'll get it done," said Eddie. They had to deliver what they had promised.

After Analise left, the boys flopped into folding chairs.

"I guess we should have planned for extra supplies," said Eddie. "Even lemonade stands need to buy more lemonade."

"This is harder than I thought it would be," said Jax.

Caleb's dad gave them a

thumbs-up through the garage-door window.

But it was more of a thumbs-down kind of day.

The boys met back at Caleb's house on Friday.

"My dad said he'd take us to the store for purple tape," said Jax.

"I have another idea," said Eddie. "Mrs. Mohan gave us boxes. Maybe she'd let us clean some more to trade for tape."

It sounded like a pretty good

idea. But it meant more cleaning and less building. And the boys were running out of time.

When they got to her house, there was rustling in the garage.

"Hello?" Caleb walked up the driveway. Jax and Eddie followed.

A girl with long, dark hair popped up from behind a shelf.

"Hi," said the girl. "My grandma is inside. She's making **laddoos**."

The boys took a good sniff of the air. They didn't know what laddoos were, but they sure smelled delicious.

"I'm **Kiara**." The girl stepped forward.

"Oh, you're the granddaughter who builds things with boxes," said Jax. "She told us about you."

"That's me." Kiara wiped her hands on her shirt. "I was just finishing up a project."

Behind her was a model of a house. A little sign next to it said DESIGN BY KIARA PAL.

"You made that?" asked Eddie. **"It's amazing!"**

Kiara smiled. "Thanks. I like to design things," she said. "And

I love coming to Nani's house because she lets me build whatever I want."

Kiara walked over to a table. **"Hey, is this yours?"** She held up one of their signs.

"Yeah, that's us," said Caleb. "But we're having a little trouble. Our first customer wants a bunch of changes."

"We were hoping your grandma would give us some of her tape if we helped her again," said Jax. He pointed to the three rolls of duct tape on the wall. Silver, black, and green.

"There's no purple, though," said Eddie.

"You need purple tape?" Kiara got up and went straight for a plastic bin. She lifted the top.

"That's Nani's tape," she said, pointing to the wall. "*This* is my tape."

The boys got up to look. It was full of duct tape!

Blue.

Orange.

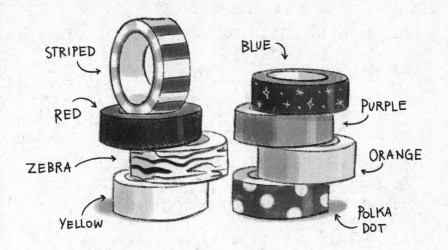

Yellow.

Red.

Striped.

Zebra.

Polka dot.

PURPLE.

"Will you trade us for the tape?"
asked Jax.

Kiara thought for a moment. "You need more than tape. It'll fix this problem, but not the next," said Kiara. "You need someone to help you plan each project."

"What do you mean?" asked Caleb.

"You can't just build like it's for you," she said. "Your customers want to know what they're getting."

"They're getting a fort," said Eddie. "It's right in our name."

Kiara nodded. "Right. But you can make an official design and have them agree to it. Any changes will cost extra."

Caleb knew she was right. "That makes sense," he said. "But we don't know anyone who can make a design."

Kiara laughed. "You do now," she said with a smile. "I've learned some things from my mom. She helps people plan their designs. She's an **architect**."

"You'd do that for us?" asked Jax.

"Sure," said Kiara. "I want to be

part of the team. Plus, I'm saving for a new design app."

"Equal partners, then," said Jax. **"Everyone agree?"**

"That's fair," said Eddie.

Caleb held out his hand. "Welcome to Team Fort Builders."

5

Making a Plan

Back in Caleb's garage, Kiara walked around the fort.

She took a piece of paper and made a sketch for the castle. She listed which box sizes they would need to finish it. She made an

estimate of how much tape would be used.

After a while, she showed everyone what she'd done.

"Wow. You're really good at this," said Eddie.

"Thanks." Kiara smiled at her creation.

"Let's move this out into the driveway," said Caleb.

It took a few pulls and pushes to get it to the middle of the driveway.

They carefully removed all the tape and took the box fort apart.

They were pretty much starting from scratch.

With Kiara's design and Jax's building skills, they got to work.

"The tower goes in front on the left," said Kiara.

"But then it's in the way of the drawbridge," said Jax.

Kiara checked her design. "We'll have to move the drawbridge to get it how Analise wants it."

"We worked really hard on this drawbridge." Jax crossed his arms.

"I know, but she wants it to go up and down, right?" asked Kiara.

Eddie and Caleb stopped picking up boxes. They didn't want anyone arguing, but they didn't know what to do either.

"Yes, but that's another hour of work to redo the drawbridge," said Jax. "And we have no time."

"That's why we made a plan," said Kiara. "You're supposed to follow the design."

"We wouldn't have needed a plan if she didn't ask for changes," Jax snapped back.

Caleb stepped in. "You guys. We're a team here."

Kiara and Jax stopped and both took a deep breath.

"Okay, give me a minute," said

Kiara. She erased and sketched. "If we put the tower in the back, you won't have to move the drawbridge."

Jax moved next to her and studied the design. "Good idea," he said.

"Great, let's get this thing done," said Caleb.

"Where's the tape?" asked Jax. It wasn't where he'd left it.

All around the fort was a big mess of tape and supplies.

"Where's the tape?" he asked again.

The four of them searched through the mess. Finally, Eddie raised his hand, holding a roll of tape. **"Found it!"** he shouted.

But just as they were about to get back to work, Jax's twin sisters showed up.

"What are you guys doing?" asked **Amber**.

"Yeah, what are you guys doing?" echoed **Dove**.

Jax pulled at the duct tape. **"We're working,"** he said. "Go play, okay?"

"We want to work," said Amber.

"Yeah, we want to work," echoed Dove.

Kiara handed the girls a box. "Can you put this on top of that box for me?"

The girls took the box. But they had other ideas.

Before everything was taped together, they were crawling through the fort.

"Stop!" shouted Jax. "You're going to—"

But it was too late.

Everything was already tumbling down!

Jax chased his little sisters to the backyard. His yell was clear from the front. "Mom! They're ruining our fort!"

Caleb took charge.

"We have less than a day left to build this fort," he said. "Let's get back to work."

They used Kiara's design to rebuild, again.

Box by box.

At first, Eddie was in charge of

supplies, but he kept losing them.

Jax was putting boxes together, but they needed him to build.

Kiara ripped the tape, but she had to have it perfect, so it was taking way too long.

And Caleb couldn't find his checklist.

"Team!" Caleb yelled.

Everyone stopped what they were doing.

"This isn't working," he said. "We should each use our skills."

He lifted his foot to get the

piece of paper that was stuck to his sneaker. It was his checklist.

"Here's the new plan," he said. "Eddie, you put the boxes together. I'll measure the tape. Jax, you stack the boxes. And Kiara, you can attach everything together."

He took the design from Kiara and taped it to the front of a box. "All supplies and lists go here. This is home base."

Caleb was really good at managing the team.

"Okay," said Jax. "All in." He

put his hand out, and one by one the others put theirs on top.

"'Go, team' on three," said Eddie.

"One, two, three," they all counted. "Go, team!"

They got right to work, doing the jobs they were best at.

A couple hours later, they were almost done.

"Did you feel that?" asked Eddie.

"Feel what?" asked Caleb.

But he got his answer quickly. Rain started coming down fast!

"We have to move the fort!" shouted Kiara.

"Grab that side," Jax said to Eddie and Caleb. "Kiara, get the home base box!"

The twins came running out front. "It's raining! It's raining!"

"Grab that last box," Jax yelled to them as the team carried the fort to the garage.

But instead of carrying the box, the girls used it as an umbrella.

6

Teamwork!

They stood in Caleb's garage as the rain poured down. Half of Analise's castle fort was a soggy, crumbling mess. The paint was running down the sides, and the tape was peeling off.

"Now what?" asked Caleb. How could they finish it in time? The party was the next day!

"We're out of boxes," said Eddie with a glum look on his face.

"And we're almost out of paint," said Jax.

"Our model fort and sign are destroyed too," Eddie pointed out.

They had come so close!

Kiara took the paper with the design and grabbed a pencil. "We can fix this. Give me a minute."

They waited as she drew.

"We only need two more boxes if we do it this way," she explained. "And Eddie can draw pink stones on the sides so we don't need a lot more paint."

"We don't have more boxes," Eddie reminded her.

"I have a plan," said Kiara. "I just need to get to Nani's house."

Caleb handed an umbrella to Kiara. "I'll go with you," he said.

They ran up Mrs. Mohan's

driveway, into the garage.

"We took all the boxes yester-day," said Caleb.

Kiara gave him a sly smile. "You took all the *empty* boxes." She went to the door and called inside. "Nani, can we empty a couple boxes for our fort? We'll **replace** them."

"Of course," answered Nani. "Put everything on the shelf for now."

Caleb and Kiara began empty-ing the boxes.

Caleb let out a sigh. "Running a business is harder than I thought. I guess my new book will have to wait."

"Which book?" asked Kiara.

"The first Castle Quest," he

answered. He took blankets out of the box in front of him. **"It's a special edition."**

"That's a great goal," said Kiara.

The boxes were ready, but it was still pouring outside.

"What if it doesn't stop raining?" asked Caleb. But neither of them had an answer.

Could they finish Analise's dream fort in time for the party?

The Fort Builders team met at Caleb's house Saturday morning.

After a night of thunderstorms, the sun was finally shining.

"We have a fort to build!" said Caleb.

They quickly got to work.

Jax and Eddie tore down the parts of the fort that had been destroyed. Kiara and Caleb got the new boxes ready.

"This box will be for the new tower," said Kiara. "The other one will be for the drawbridge and the extra window."

While Jax and Caleb attached

the tower, Kiara and Eddie outlined what they needed cut. **Mr.
Rivers** came out to **supervise**.

"We're going to need a lot of
tape," said Jax.

The team worked hard to piece
it all together.

They used every scrap of cardboard they had left.

"Kiara and I will finish the
drawbridge," said Caleb.

"And we'll paint," said
Jax. He handed Eddie a brush.

They sang as they worked.

They even danced a little.

Caleb made holes on each side of the castle door. He made two more on the drawbridge. Kiara poked the rope through and knotted all the ends.

Eddie and Jax used every last drop of paint.

Finally, it was done!

The pink castle with purple tape was finished, and it looked amazing!

When Analise got to Caleb's house at noon with her dad, the

garage door was closed. The Fort Builders crew was waiting on the porch for her.

"I got your message," she said. "I'm so excited to see it!"

They stood in front of the garage door for the big **reveal**.

Caleb handed Analise the garage door remote. "Go ahead. Press the button," he said.

Analise pressed it. She waited eagerly as the door inched up. **"It's beautiful!"** she yelled. She ran right over to the fort.

"I guess that means you like it?" asked Jax, laughing.

"Like it? I love it!" Analise hugged the side.

They showed her how to work the drawbridge. And the secret entry they'd added to the back, like a tunnel.

"Will you tell your friends about our business?" asked Caleb.

"Of course!" said Analise. "You built me my dream fort!"

There it was. The perfect quote for their advertising.

Analise handed Caleb ten dollars, as promised. The team carefully loaded the fort onto the back of Mr. Stevens's truck. They waved as they rode down the street to Analise's house.

"We did it," said Caleb. "I'll go get some change so we can split this. Meet me on the porch."

But when he went inside, Jax, Eddie, and Kiara made a different plan.

Caleb came back out and reached into his pocket. "Here's your share of the profits." He handed each of them two dollars and fifty cents.

They all smiled weird smiles. Sneaky smiles.

"What?" asked Caleb. "I know it's not enough for what we wanted, but we'll get more customers."

Jax laughed. "It's enough," he said. He held the money out to Caleb.

Eddie and Kiara did the same.

"What are you talking about?" asked Caleb.

"This all started because of you," said Eddie.

"And we think you should get that book you want," added Jax.

"But—" Caleb started.

"But nothing," said Kiara. "You earned it. We'll get our stuff when we get more jobs."

"Are you sure?" Caleb asked. They were being so **generous.**

"We're sure!" they all said at once.

A big smile lit up Caleb's face. **"Thank you! You guys are the best!"**

Caleb would finally have his special-edition copy of Castle Quest. But *best* of all, he had become part of a team. And who knew what the Fort Builders team could accomplish next?

Word List

advertise (AD•vur•tize):
Provide information and draw
attention to goods or a service

architect (AR•kih•tekt):
Someone who designs buildings

displayed (dihs•PLAYD):
Showed or put out to view

estimate (ESS•tih•miht): An
educated guess

generous (JEN•ur•uhss):
Willing to give and share

laddoos (luh•DOOZ): An Indian

dessert made of flour, sugar, and ghee, butter, or oil

motto (MAHT•toh): A phrase that states the mission of a business

official (uh•FI•shull): Approved by authority

profits (PRAHF•itz): The money made after costs are paid

replace (rih•PLAYSE): To restore what was taken

reveal (rih•VEEL): A show of what was hidden

supervise (SOO•pur•vize): To oversee a task

Questions

1. Why did Caleb and Jax want to start their fort-building business? Did they get what they wanted in the end? Why or why not?

2. What did the Fort Builders group learn about working together as a team? Why is teamwork important?

3. What kind of business would you like to start? What would you name it?

STEM Activity

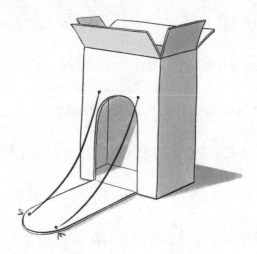

How to build a drawbridge:

Step 1: Starting at the bottom of a cardboard box, draw a closed drawbridge. It can be arched or rectangular.

Step 2: With the help of an adult, cut along the lines, leaving the bottom attached to form a hinge.

Step 3: Use a screwdriver to make one small hole on each side of the drawbridge and one small hole on each side above the doorway.

Step 4: Cut two pieces of string or rope (about twice the length of the drawbridge). Feed them through from the drawbridge to the doorway on each side. While the drawbridge is open, tie knots to secure the rope behind all four holes.

Step 5: Pull the ropes to raise and lower your drawbridge.

Step 6: Have fun!